D0271198

This picture book belongs to

. . . .

For Ramona
who tells stories and makes jokes
and quite possibly sings songs.
S.P.

For my dad and the sisters
Nan, Olive and Winnie. Miss you lots.
A.B.

COVENTRY SCHOOLS LIBRARY SERVICE	
20-Sep-01	JF
PETERS	

First published in Great Britain 2001
by Egmont Children's Books Limited,
a division of Egmont Holding Limited, 239 Kensington High Street, London W8 6SA

Text © Simon Puttock 2001
Illustrations © Alison Bartlett 2001
The author and illustrator have asserted their moral rights

A CIP catalogue record for this title is available from the British Library

0 7497 4022 1

10 9 8 7 6 5 4 3 2 1
Printed in U.A.E

A Story for Hippo

Simon Puttock

illustrated by Alison Bartlett

EGMONT CHILDREN'S BOOKS

Hippo was the oldest and wisest of all the animals. She lived on the bank of the wide, blue river and told the most wonderful stories.

Monkey was not as old or as wise as Hippo. To tell the truth, Monkey was a bit of a joker. He could make the whole forest laugh with his antics.

Monkey lived on the bank of the wide, blue river with Hippo.

Each evening, as the forest was falling asleep, Hippo told Monkey stories.

"Which story would you like tonight, Monkey? Would you like the one about the three-headed giant?"

"Well . . . perhaps," said Monkey.

"Or the one about the princess and the moon?"

"Well . . . maybe," said Monkey.

"I know," said Hippo, "would you like the one about you and me?"

"Yes, please!" said Monkey.

"Once upon a time," she began, "there lived a hippo and a monkey."

"Yes," said Monkey, "a big, round hippo, and a middle-sized monkey."

"Exactly," Hippo laughed. "And they were best friends."

"Best, best, best friends," said Monkey.

"And they told stories and ate cabbages."
"And coconuts, too," said Monkey, who loved coconuts.

"And coconuts, too," Hippo agreed. "And they played games–"

"And ran races!" Monkey butted in again.

"Oh, Monkey," Hippo laughed. "This hippo was too slowed down and old to run races. But even so, and day by day, they both lived happily ever after."

"Oh, yes," said Monkey contentedly. "That is a good story."

Little Chameleon lived under a leaf on the bank of the wide, blue river. She listened to Hippo's stories and laughed at Monkey's jokes, but she was shy and she stayed beneath her leaf, though she longed to join in. If I were brave enough, she thought, I would sing them a song. Little Chameleon loved to sing.

One evening Hippo said, "Monkey, I am very old."

"Yes," agreed Monkey, "too old for races and wise as wise can be."

"And I am very, very tired," said Hippo, "and I always knew that, like all old hippos, one day I would have to die."

"No!" said Monkey,
feeling scared.
"You cannot!
If you die, who will
tell the most wonderful
stories? Who will
laugh at my jokes?"
"Everybody laughs at
your jokes," said Hippo.
"But you laugh loudest,"
said Monkey.
"Please don't die, Hippo."

Hippo smiled.
"Everyone must die
some day, Monkey.
Nobody knows how to
live forever, not even
a wise old hippo."

"Then happily ever after isn't true," said Monkey. He was angry because Hippo was leaving him.

"But Monkey," said Hippo, "I have lived happily ever after. I have had the best and funniest friend in all the forest and a long and happy life.

You will find new friends, tell new jokes and hear new stories. You will enjoy the days and dream the nights away and you will live happily ever after, too."

Hippo paused for a moment.
"Will you forget me, Monkey?"
she asked softly.

"Of course I won't forget you," shouted Monkey. "You're my best, best, best friend." "Thank you," said Hippo. "Because that will be part of my happily ever after."

And Hippo went away into the jungle's deepest shade where all the hippos go when it is time for them to die.

Monkey missed Hippo. Day after day he sat by the river and wept. He decided he would never tell jokes again.

The forest was silent and sad.

Everyone missed Hippo and everyone missed Monkey's antics.

One evening, when the forest was falling asleep, Little Chameleon crept out from under her leaf. She could not bear to hear Monkey crying any more.

"Tell me a joke," she said, "I want
to laugh."

"Go away," said Monkey, "I can't!
I won't!"

"Then tell me a story, please," said
Little Chameleon.

"I haven't any stories," said Monkey.

"Yes you do," said Little Chameleon.
"You have all the stories Hippo told."

"But they belonged to Hippo," said Monkey, drying his eyes.

"They are your stories now," said Little Chameleon, "and stories need to be told."

"But I miss Hippo," said Monkey.

"I miss her too," said Little Chameleon. "Please, tell me a story with Hippo inside it."

Monkey sniffed a soggy sniff. "All right, I'll try."

"Once upon a
time," he began,
"there lived a
little chameleon
and a monkey."

"That's a good beginning,"
said Little Chameleon.

"And they missed Hippo very much."

"That's true," said
Little Chameleon sadly.

"But Little Chameleon and Monkey told each other stories, and laughed at each other's jokes, and . . ." Monkey paused for a moment.

"And sang songs," said
Little Chameleon, who
had a beautiful voice
and used to sing
the most wonderful
songs alone
beneath her leaf.

" . . . and
sang songs,"
Monkey agreed,
"and after a while
they lived happily
ever after."

"That is a good story," said Little Chameleon, curling up contentedly on her leaf.

"Now, tell me another."

3 8002 00949 9098

MADE BY EGMONT

HANDLED WITH CARE

Books are great! And these ones prove it. goose Wolf

Koala and the Flower *by Mary Murphy*
0 7497 4407 3

Mr Wolf's Pancakes *by Jan Fearnley*
0 7497 3559 7

Cat's Colours *by Jane Cabrera*
0 7497 3120 6

Dog's Day *by Jane Cabrera*
0 7497 4392 1

I wish I were a dog *by Lydia Monks*
0 7497 3803 0

The Three Little Wolves and the Big Bad Pig
by Eugene Trivizas and Helen Oxenbury
0 7497 2505 2

And they're all only £4.99